Terror

By Day

Terror By Day

Day

Dr. Bo Wagner

Word of His Mouth Publishers
Mooresboro, NC

All Scripture quotations are taken from the **King James Version** of the Bible.

ISBN: 978-1-941039-10-6

Printed in the United States of America
©2019 Dr. Bo Wagner

Word of His Mouth Publishers
Mooresboro, NC 28114
www.wordofhismouth.com

Cover art by Chip Nuhrah

Chapter One

Adventure? I don't think so...

Knife-wielding Indians? That would be a "no," along with pirates, Nazis, treacherous Mayans, and filthy, smarmy slave traders.

Oh, and no demon posing as a "Moth Man" either.

Nope, this week would be radically different for us adventurous Night Heroes. This week would be sun, fun, relaxation, snorkeling, family time, and all the food we could possibly eat.

That's right; the entire Warner family was going on our first ever cruise. Our family vacation this year would take us from the port of Charleston, down the coast of the eastern seaboard, and then to the Bahamas.

And boy, oh boy, did my sisters and I need the break!

I know what you must be thinking, "Why would a bunch of kids need a vacation?" Of course, you are probably also thinking, "What in the world is he babbling about? What kid in our modern world is worried about Indians or pirates or Nazis or slave traders or, what was it, "Moth Men?"

Perhaps a bit of explanation is in order. We, my two sisters and I, are not quite ordinary kids:

We are the Night Heroes.

My dad is an evangelist. He travels all around the country and the world preaching the gospel, telling everyone about Jesus. My mom and sisters and I travel everywhere with him.

A couple of years ago, while my dad was preaching in the tiny town of Boomer, West Virginia, the strangest thing happened. Here is how I described it in our first book, The Cry from the Coal Mine:

> "For most folks, sleeping in a strange new place would be hard. But when you do it most of the year, after a while you get used to it. So, we settled down, took time to read our Bibles, which we all love, and then mom and dad came in and prayed with us. They left the room, turning off the lights as they left, and we closed our eyes and adjusted to the new sounds

around us. I could hear the air conditioner kicking in. I could hear a car or two going down the road headed in the direction of Smithers. I could hear crickets from somewhere outside. I could hear the sound of a train whistle. And then I heard the conductor of the train call out three names: 'Kyle! Carrie! Aly!'

"I sat straight up in bed. I looked to my left, and Carrie was sitting straight up in bed too. Same for Aly on my right. Only none of us were in bed anymore. We were all sitting on the front porch of an old railroad depot, and the sun was just coming up over the mountain behind us. In front of us sat an old train, with smoke belching from the engine in the front. Past the train was a river, and on the other side of the river another track for trains, and just past that a very high mountain, meaning that we were in a deep valley. The conductor stood staring at us as if he expected us to do something. For our part, we were looking back and forth from each other to him to the train to the river and back to each other again, wondering which one of us was dreaming. Finally, the conductor spoke again. 'Kyle, Carrie, Aly. Climb aboard, he needs your help.'

"It's hard to explain what we all felt right then. Talking about it later, it was like a mixture of being scared, being curious, and wanting to laugh at how silly it all seemed yet being amazed at how real it all felt. We sat there, unsure of what to do, and then the conductor spoke again. 'Warner children, come aboard this train this instant. You are here for a reason, and the night is waning fast. You have only five nights here to help him, and every moment lost will make it that much harder to do so. Your mother and father have taught you to help those in need, and this boy's need is dire. So once again, please come aboard.'

" 'With all due respect, sir,' said my sister Carrie, 'we don't know you, and we don't even know how we got here. The last thing I remember is going to sleep. It is now quite clearly *daytime*, and yet you just said that the *night* was waning fast. Are we dreaming?'

" 'You obviously listen very carefully, young lady, and you are very perceptive. That is one of the reasons you children have been summoned here tonight, or today, depending upon your perspective. To answer your question, yes, you are dreaming, but no, you are not dreaming like you might think. You will wake up in the morning in your beds in the guest room, and you will be rested from a night of sleep, but what is happening right now here in this daytime is very real. Every decision you make will have an impact, and precious lives are hanging in the balance. Now please climb aboard; we are wasting very valuable time.'

"My sisters and I looked at each other, still a bit unsure. It was little Aly who finally settled the issue. 'Look,' she said, her hazel eyes peeping out from under blonde bangs, 'what do we have to lose? If this isn't a dream, then we obviously are not where we should be, and maybe this train will take us back. But if it is a dream, then whatever we do, we'll eventually wake up anyway. But if the conductor is right, and some little boy needs us, how could we ever live with ourselves if we don't help him?' "

We ended up rescuing that boy from the very bad men that had him trapped. We learned some valuable things, such as the fact that whatever we go to sleep with in our time, we can carry back with us into the past. That has turned out to be very helpful on many occasions.

We went on from there to rescue a little girl from a concentration camp in Nazi Germany of World War II, and we stopped two brothers from killing each other during the Civil War battle of Chickamauga. We rescued a boy who was about to be killed by a hotheaded, knife-wielding Indian near Rogersville, Tennessee, we dealt with an off-his-rocker psychotic pirate terrorizing a small North Carolina town, and we unraveled a Mayan mystery in Hiawassee, Georgia. We then had the spiritual battle of our lives against the legendary "Moth Man" of Point Pleasant, West Virginia, and we rescued a sweet lady from being sold away from her husband by a jerk slave owner in Walterboro, South Carolina.

Now you know why we need a vacation!

I looked up into the front seat of our trusty old Yukon and saw my dad, the well-known evangelist, Mr. Impatience, already beginning to unwind. The normal "we have a schedule to keep and must be early for all of it" grimace was giving way to an "I can almost feel the sea breezes from here" smile.

Seated beside him in the passenger seat was mom, the greatest lady alive, and she was also already slipping into vacation mode. Normally, she would have a computer or tablet in her lap working, but at the moment, she had just a book. And not a study book either. No, if I saw the reflection right, it was *The Prudent Queen*, a historical fiction novel about Queen Esther written by Angela W. Buff, a truly phenomenal writer.

Beside me, behind mom, was the middle Warner brat (as our folks lovingly call us) Carrie, my dark-haired, serious-minded, fourteen-year-old certified genius of a sister. Like mom, her nose was buried in a book as well. I could not help but shake my head and grin as I read the cover of the massive book with a black cover:

The Rise and Fall of the Third Reich by William Shirer.

Yep, that's my sister. I would have asked her why she didn't do some "pleasure reading," but I knew she would just have stared at me blankly, since for her, a huge history book actually is pleasure reading.

I looked over my shoulder into the back seat to see what the third Night Hero, my recently turned thirteen-year-old, blonde-haired sister Aly was doing, and, true to form, she did not disappoint.

Little Miss "Lightning in a Bottle" was making a hideous face at some random kid in a vehicle in the lane beside us.

"Yo, Pipsqueak," I hissed quietly, "what in the world are you doing?"

"Shhhh," she hissed back as she looked over at me, "don't break my concentration. Me and this twerp have been going at it for miles, and he is going to give up any minute now."

I could not help but laugh.

"Um, Sis, I don't think so. Look."

She turned back to face her adversary, and found that he was holding a hand-scrawled sign up to face her:

U R

Weird

Her mouth dropped open, her eyes got wide, and the kid in the other car stuck his tongue out at her as they pulled off at an exit.

"You lost that one, Sis, big time."

She just harumphed.

Yep, this was going to be an epic week. And above all, a relaxing week, I was quite sure of it.

Chapter Two

In all of my sixteen years thus far, nothing had really prepared me for the sight of the massive Atlantic Queen cruise ship. I looked at the huge ropes holding her to the dock, then looked down at my own decent size muscles that had not too long back climbed an anchor chain to get aboard a pirate ship.

"Nope, even with my above-average strength, I don't think I would want to try and climb that," I mumbled.

In the front seat, mom and dad were conversing about where exactly to go. The sign system for parking and unloading was, to put it mildly, a bit insufficient. Finally, we found the place to stop and unload the luggage, and then we three kids and mom took it out of the vehicle, and a porter loaded it onto a cart while dad went and parked the vehicle in the cruise line parking lot a few blocks away.

Five minutes later, we were reunited and happily walking toward the building which would be the entry port for the ship. I was as light as a feather and as relaxed as a beach bum...

Right up until I saw the security checkpoints.

Each and every person going on to the ship had to go through a metal detector first, show a passport, and show one other form of ID. There were two fairly serious and stout looking security guards overseeing the entire operation. I don't really know why, but somehow all of that really tensed me up.

Apparently, I wasn't the only one.

"Dad," Aly asked with concern in her voice, "is all of that really necessary? This is a cruise ship, not a warship."

"It is more necessary than if it were a warship, baby," he said. "There will be three thousand vacationers on this ship, all of them unarmed. There are some very bad people in this world, and if any of them happened to get on one of these ships, this could go from being a vacation to the world's largest burial at sea."

Sobering thought.

But it didn't last long. We got through security very quickly and made our way up into the ship. We made a quick right, hopped in the elevator, and made our way up to the eighth deck.

And when the elevator opened, every Warner's jaw dropped, and all ten of our eyes opened wider than you would ever think possible.

It looked like we had walked into a mansion.

All of us said it at once, "Whoooaaaaaa."

We were right at the very center of the ship. We walked over to the railings, and I almost got lightheaded. I looked down and saw seven decks below me. The deck we came in on and the one below that was off-limits except for embarking and disembarking. I looked up and saw three more floors above me.

"We could skydive in here, Bro!" Aly whispered to me.

I just grinned. She was not too far off from being right.

The glass elevator we were standing beside made its way slowly up and down from floor to floor. There was also a regal looking, lighted, crystal-encrusted, winding staircase that went from bottom to top.

There were restaurants on every floor, game rooms on most floors, shops and stores everywhere, and I knew we were only seeing the tip of the iceberg (pardon the Titanic reference) of all the ship had to offer. It was basically a floating city complete with thousands of rooms, more kinds of food than one could possibly try in a week, enough entertainment to keep anyone from ever getting bored, medical facilities in case anyone got hurt, a gymnasium to work out in, swimming pools and hot tubs, it was almost overwhelming.

"What shall we do first, sweetheart?" Dad asked mom.

"I'm thinking food," she said with a smile.

"Yes!" Aly shouted as she bent over, balled up her fist, and punched the air with it three or four times. "That's what I'm talking about!"

All of us busted out laughing, and then mom led the way toward a restaurant at the back of the boat. None of us had to ask how she knew where it was; mom always researched every location before we arrived. I had no doubt in my mind that even having never been on that boat, she could make her way through it to any location blindfolded.

Chapter Three

It had only been an hour ago that all of us were hungry. Famished, really, after the long drive. But not a single Warner was hungry at the moment. In fact, for a fleeting moment, I wondered if any of us would ever be hungry again.

Yes, we ate that much at lunch.

"I'm about to pop," dad said with a groan.

"Would that make you a 'Pop Pop?'" Carrie quipped.

"Ohhh, don't make me laugh; my stomach can't handle it," mom said with a grin.

We had eaten cheeseburgers, pizza, French fries, mom and dad each had a salad to go along with that, and everyone had dessert. The lunch was self-serve from seven different buffet bars in the restaurant. And boy had we self-served...

Dad pushed away from the table, interlaced his fingers, put his hands over his head and stretched, cracking his fingers.

"Okay, family, we have a long and amazing week ahead of us. But I would recommend we go out on deck to begin with. The ship should be pulling out of port in about fifteen minutes, and that is a sight that you don't want to miss."

All of us joined him in pushing away from the table, and we started meandering deeper into the restaurant, which we knew would come out on the very back deck of the boat. Dad pushed open the door and held it for mom first and all of the rest of us next, and I was reminded again how important it is for a young man to be a gentleman. A young man who is a gentleman will probably grow up to be a husband and father who is a gentleman, but a young man who thinks only of himself is not likely to change as he gets older.

All of us cleared the door, dad let it close behind us, and we made our way to the edge of the ship.

As we looked down at the dock, we saw two men untying the gigantic ropes and tossing them into the water. As soon as they splashed down, an engine started vibrating below us, and we saw the ropes being sucked into the ship like giant strands of spaghetti.

Three minutes later, they were clear, and we felt a much deeper rumbling from somewhere in the bowels of the ship. The ship, oh so slowly, started to move away from the dock, gathered speed as it went, and in very short order, the port of Charleston began to fade from view.

"Babe, we are on vacation," dad said as he grinned at mom. Then he leaned over and kissed her, and Aly immediately gave her standard "Ewwww, gross."

Mom grinned down at her and said, "One day, you won't think so."

Aly just rolled her eyes, dad took mom by the hand, and they started leading the way to our rooms.

The sleeping arrangements this week would be a bit unique for us. Cruise ships do not normally have very many rooms suitable for large families, so instead of one room, we would have two rooms side by side with a door that can open between them.

Mom and dad's room had one king-size bed, a little balcony, a tiny bathroom, and almost no walking space. Our room had a tiny sleeper couch and two beds that folded down out of the walls to go along with our tiny bathroom, little balcony, and almost no walking space.

The luggage had arrived ahead of us, and we spent the next little while getting everything organized inside the rooms. When space is that tight, good organization is a must.

Once we had everything set up like we wanted it, instinctively, all five of us gravitated to the two little balconies. We plopped down in the little plastic chairs and stared out in awe at the beauty of God's creation. And as if the beautiful water was not amazing enough, a school of dolphins was shadowing us and jumping out of the water as they did!

I am telling you, God is good.

For the next couple of hours, we all just rested. Mom went and laid on their bed to read, Carrie and Aly did the same thing in our room, and dad and I just sat on the balconies and propped our feet up on the chairs the ladies had vacated. And as we all rested in our own unique ways, I could not help but be reminded that rest itself is a gift from the hand of our very good God. Mark 6:31 says, "And he (Jesus) said unto them, Come ye yourselves apart into a desert place, and rest a while: for there were many coming and going, and they had no leisure so much as to eat."

Yes, even active kids can enjoy rest.
But only for so long.

Who knew that cruise ships have putt-putt courses on top? Dad, that's who. And at the moment we five Warners were in a death match of a putt-putt game, with Mom in the lead, Dad one stroke behind, and Carrie and Aly and I tied at three strokes back.

"I'm comin' for ya, Pop Pop," Aly teased as she took aim for her next shot.

"Seriously? Are we not going to let that one go?" Dad said in pretend frustration. That is one thing I really love about my dad; he is not stuffy. We kids respect him, but he is not too serious to laugh at himself or to let others do so.

Aly swung the putter, and her ball rushed down the tiny fairway. It bounced hard against the corner angle, and then careened completely off of our hole and onto a different one entirely!

In his mock sorrowful voice, dad said, "Awww, did Pookie Wookie hit the ball too hard? Is her sad sad that her is going to lose to dad again, for like the bazillionth time?"

Aly gritted her teeth and growled at him, and all of the rest of us laughed hysterically. Nicely played, dad, nicely played.

To make an eighteen-hole-long story short, Dad and mom ended up tying for first, Carrie came in second ("It's all physics," she kept reminding us), I finished one shot behind her, and "Pookie Wookie," who never did recover from her disaster, finished a very distant last.

And that all made for great teasing at supper.

Yes, we all recovered our appetites in time for supper, and I am so glad we did!

The Star of the Sea may well be the best restaurant I have ever eaten at in my young life. But it was very, very different from the self-serve buffet at lunch.

When we walked in, the very official looking gentleman in the tuxedo said, "Welcome, Mr. and Mrs. Warner, and welcome to you as well, Kyle, Carrie, and Aly."

The man knew us by name! We had never met him in our lives, and he knew us by name. I knew that he must have studied the pictures of everyone on the boat, and somehow he knew who everyone was just by sight.

Another man in a tuxedo, holding a towel over one arm, said, "Follow me, please," and started leading the way into the restaurant. Like the restaurant at lunch, it was in the back of the ship, but it was one deck higher.

As we weaved through the other tables and patrons, we passed lovely ice sculptures, live plants that I had never even seen before, and walked under crystal chandeliers. We arrived at our table, and the man with the towel pulled mom's chair out and allowed her to sit. All of us were on our own on that one.

"Samir will be your server tonight, sirs and madams," he said officiously. Then he bowed his head slightly to us, turned, and went to lead the next folks to their table.

"Wow," Carrie said with wide eyes and a smile, "I never thought we would be getting this kind of treatment! I mean, church potlucks week after week are nice and everything, but..."

Her voice trailed off, and mom finished her thought for her.

"But paper plates and plastic silverware don't quite compare to fine china and crystal glasses! But," she said with that sweet smile that all of us loved so much, "those potlucks served on paper plates are made by God's people, the very best people on earth, and they are made solely out of love, not as a business venture."

All of us just nodded. There was no need to add anything to that, she said it all, and she said it right.

After a happy minute or so of small talk, Samir arrived, bringing each of us a glass of ice water. He had dark skin, black as night hair, and almost black eyes so common to Middle Easterners. He looked to be about thirty, and even through his tuxedo shirt, I could see that he was every bit as muscular and powerful as my dad.

I didn't see that every day, not at all.

"Good evening Mr. and Mrs. Warner and children," he said pleasantly. His teeth were as white as a field of snow, and he seemed to genuinely enjoy being there.

"What may I offer you to drink? For the adults, we have a lovely selection of wine to begin with."

I knew what was coming and coming immediately.

"Thank you, Samir, but we do not drink alcohol. I will have an unsweetened tea with plenty of ice."

Mom ordered a water, I got a sweet tea, and each of the girls asked for soft drinks. Samir bowed slightly, just as the man with the towel had done, smiled that bright smile again, and made his way toward the kitchen to get our drinks.

While he was gone, a lady arrived at our table carrying a basket of freshly baked bread and a tray of real butter. Real butter, I tell you, not margarine, not butter substitute, butter.

I. Love. Butter.

I started to reach for the loaf to cut myself a slice and was instantly reminded how fast my mom is and has been since as far back as I can remember.

Whap! She popped my hand, and startled, I yanked it back. Then everyone laughed; they knew what I had forgotten. Without anyone having to say anything, five Warners all joined hands in a circle around the round table and bowed our heads, and dad began to pray aloud.

"Dear Father, thank you so much for allowing us to be here as a family. You have given us the blessing of serving you together as I travel and preach, and now you give us the blessing of having a wonderful vacation together. May it be a restful one, Lord. Thank you so much for the food that you have provided us, may it be a nourishment to our bodies. We pray this in the name above all names, the matchless name of Jesus, amen."

All of us echoed our own "Amen" and raised our heads.

When we did, all of us jerked a bit. Samir was standing right at our table. He had arrived during our prayer and had done it so very quietly that we had not even known he was there. We smiled up at him...

And he did not smile in return. Not a single one of those snow-white teeth were showing. His entire face seemed to have changed, actually, and his demeanor was very strange, sort of strained, I guess. He set the drinks down in their proper places and proceeded to take all of our food orders. Then he bowed his head slightly once again and disappeared to the kitchen.

Whatever his problem was, it did not register with me for long at all. Everyone has issues, I guess. But what I had was a plate of steak and lobster in front of me. As did Dad, Mom, Carrie, and Aly. Yes, there were other choices on the menu, lots of them. But when steak and lobster are one of the choices, is there really a need to choose anything else?

Of course, we also had salads, baked potatoes, soup, and dessert.

About the time the dessert arrived, we had a very distinguished-looking gentleman in a nautical looking hat come over to our table and speak to us.

"Welcome to the Atlantic Queen," he said pleasantly, "I do hope you folks are enjoying yourselves thus far."

Dad, who easily recognized the significance of his hat and the insignia on his arm, said, "Yes sir, Mr. Captain, we are enjoying ourselves immensely. This is a lovely boat you have."

"Thank you so much; that is so kind of you to say. It took me thirty years to get to this point; I was on much smaller vessels when I began my sailing career. But I always had this one thing in mind, captaining the big boats with the most souls on board."

The Captain and my dad made small talk for a few moments, then he went on his way to speak to the other guests at the other tables.

And by the time we were all done with dessert, we were all happily miserable once again and waddled to our rooms to get a good night's sleep at sea. I had no doubt that lying down on a soft bed on the gently rocking waves was going to knock me out cold and keep me sound asleep all through the night.

And as I lay there in bed, my next to last waking thought was, "Thank you for all of this, Lord," and my very last thought, as I grinned ear to ear, was, "Not tonight, Mr. Conductor, not tonight."

Chapter Four

Do you like alarm clocks? Me neither. To me, they rank right down there with homework and zits and having to babysit kids who produce epic poopy diapers.

But there were no alarm clocks on the boat; we all got to sleep until we woke up. That is, to quote Aly, "Awweeessssoooommmme!"

It was the rumbling of my stomach that finally made me blink my eyes open. That and the fact that my head felt just a little bit funny after a night of sleeping on a boat rocking gently on the waves of the ocean.

Aly was already gone, and I was guessing she was somewhere with mom getting coffee. Carrie was on the balcony reading a book. I got up and brushed my teeth and got myself presentable for the day and then hollered out to Carrie, "Hey, Sis, let's see if we can

27

round up the folks and scrounge up some breakfast."

Carrie loves books, but she also likes eating just as much as the rest of us, so she snapped her book closed, slipped on her Crocs, and knocked on the door between our two rooms.

"Come in," dad said pleasantly. We walked in and found dad at a tiny desk with reading glasses on and his Bible in front of him.

As we have all heard him say so many times, "We may take a vacation, but we never take a vacation from God."

"I'm guessing you two are hungry," he said with a smile.

"Your guess is utterly accurate," Carrie said in a professorial tone.

"Then what say we mosey back up to the Star of the Sea, I hear their breakfast is every bit as good as their supper, and that is where your mom and Aly are already sitting down to have their morning coffee."

We didn't have to be asked twice. We vacated the room, turned left, and went down the long hallway until we were in the center of the ship, then took the glass elevator up four floors. The beautiful Atlantic sun was shining down on to the skylights above us, illuminating all of the crystal and the mirrors that seemed to be everywhere in the center of the ship.

The doors opened, we headed for the back of the boat one more time, and when we walked into the restaurant, the gentleman at the front counter once again addressed us by name and pointed us to the table where mom and Aly were sipping on their coffee.

"Glad you folks could join us," Mom said pleasantly as we arrived. "Pull up a seat."

We not only pulled up seats, we also pulled up menus. Just a few moments later, the table was crowded with steak and eggs and toast and bagels with smoked salmon. Definitely not fast food fare, that.

We casually ate, not in any particular hurry. Today would be what the cruise line calls a day at sea. We were slowly making our way down the eastern seaboard, and all we would see today is water.

There is something awesome about family times around the table. Even when we are on land, mom and dad have taught us to put a priority on those moments. No one lives forever, and everyone ought to cherish and spend time with their family while they can.

Finally, though, dad began to show his restless side. "Okay, folks, breakfast has been wonderful, but what say we get about our day? There are a jillion things to do on this boat; what does everyone have in mind?"

29

Would you believe it? A definite division of thought between the adults and the kids reared its head. While Carrie and Aly and I were saying, "Water slide!" mom was saying, "Art gallery!" And dad, who thinks mom is living art, looked over at her and said, "The artworks of the greatest masters of history don't hold a candle to you; but if you would like to go look at art that is inferior to your lovely self, I would be honored to come with you."

Blech.

But then he redeemed himself, thankfully, by turning to we three kids and saying, "But if you three would like to go to the waterslide, feel free to do so. I know I don't have to tell you this, but number one, behave yourselves, and number two, watch out for each other."

I so badly wanted to look at Carrie and Aly and grin that knowing grin, but I dared not do so. If dad only knew how many times we had watched out for each other...

"You can go," he said simply, "Just meet us for lunch at one o'clock at Sea Side Pizza."

"Yes sir!" we all chimed, then immediately we bolted up from the table and went running back for the room.

This was going to be an awesome day.

My sisters and I are a lot alike in many things, but we also each have our areas of differences. One area of similarity/difference is that when it comes time for something like a waterslide, Aly and I can be ready in two minutes flat, while Carrie will take at least fifteen minutes to get ready, mostly because she is agonizing over not being able to take her books with her. Being without her books is horrifying to her, but risking having them get wet is even more unthinkable.

Anyway, what all of that meant for this day was that Aly and I were in and out of the room in a flash, with Carrie saying words we had heard so many times before as we left, "Y'all go on ahead, I'll catch up."

And so we did.

There is something amazingly cool about a waterslide on a cruise ship on the ocean. This particular corkscrew style tube slide actually went out over the edge of the boat and was made of clear plastic where it did, so you could see the ocean down below you at that point.

It was at least three stories high, with steep steps leading up to it.

"We've climbed bigger," Aly grinned, and then she took off running for the stairs and started climbing as fast as a monkey. I fell in behind her and started making the ascent as well.

When we got to the top, she did not even hesitate as she jumped into the tube, yelling "WOOOOHOOOO!" at the top of her lungs. I dove in after her, and it felt like flying a fighter jet as I whipped around curves at breakneck speed, heading down toward the water.

Fourteen seconds. That is how long it took to whip out the bottom of the tube and "kersplash!" into the pool down below it. I came up out of the water, shook my head, rubbed my eyes, and looked around for Aly. The first thing I saw was her wide eyes and beaming face as she shouted, "That was totally wicked!"

Yep, she has not forgotten *The Incredibles*.

In a flash, she was out of the pool and heading to the stairs again, and I was on her heels. Other kids and even other adults were also starting into the line and up the steps, so it took us a little longer to get to the top and make our second slide.

And then our third. And then our fourth.

When I came up out of the water on that fourth time down, I thought of Carrie. I looked at my watch, and it had been twenty minutes since we left the room.

"Everything okay, bro?" Aly asked. "Your face has that 'concerned hero' look that I really don't want to see all week."

"Yeah, I'm sure everything's fine," I said with a shrug. "It's just that I figured Carrie would be here by now."

"Don't worry," she said as she rolled her eyes, "we're on vacation here. Everything is good, this is all sun and all fun all day, followed by the exact same thing the day after that and the day after that and the day after that. Got it?"

"Got it," I grinned, "all fun all day, followed by the exact same thing the day after that and the day after that and the day after that."

I did not know Carrie had slipped up to the pool right behind us.

"Well," she said in a very serious whisper, "if you consider drowning at sea along with three thousand other people 'fun,' then, yeah, 'all fun, all day.'"

Chapter Five

"So, give it to me again one more time, slowly," I said as the three of us sat on beach chairs by the edge of the deck far enough away from others that we were satisfied we could not be overheard.

Carrie rolled her eyes and then put her hand to her forehead and sighed heavily.

"Okay. On the way to the pool to catch up with you guys, I passed by the little chapel here on the boat. I doubt seriously if you two even noticed it as much of a hurry as you were in. But as I passed by, you know my penchant for noticing things, what I caught sight of made me do a double-take, and that led me to do some eavesdropping. I know, I know, that is rude, but I guess after all we have been through, it is sort of a hard habit to break."

"And?" Aly said simply.

"And," Carrie continued, I saw four men bowing on Muslim prayer cloths, and one of them was Samir, our waiter from yesterday who seemed to get so agitated at our prayer before the meal. That all by itself is obviously nothing to worry about. But the fact that I heard them repeatedly chanting a couple of pretty significant words is something to worry about."

"And what words would those be, Sis?" I asked, still assuming she was just overreacting.

"Jihad and antiqam."

Growing a bit more concerned, I replied, "Okay, you have me going your direction on that first word. Even a non-genius like me recognizes the word jihad. That is Islamic 'holy war on infidels,' and by infidels, they mean us. But I have never heard that second word."

"Antiqam is not as well-known of a word, but it is just as significant; it means revenge. That, combined with the name I heard them muttering and a date they were also repeating, locks it in. The name was Bin Laden, and the date was May 3, 2011."

"Okay," I said with growing concern, "Bin Laden everybody knows. As in, Osama Bin Laden, the man who masterminded the attacks on the World Trade Center in New York City on 9/11. He was later killed by U.S. special ops forces. But what in the world is May 3, 2011, about?"

"That, my dear brother, is the day that American forces buried his body at sea, infuriating the Islamic world."

My eyes got wide. Aly's got even wider.

We both got the picture, and it was not a good picture.

"They intend to avenge not just his death, but his watery grave. They are going to try to sink this ship and drown all of us," Aly said with a look of horror on her face.

Carrie nodded her head up and down slowly.

"We need to tell ship security and the captain," I said as I started to rise out of my chair.

Carrie put her hand on my arm, letting me know I needed to stay seated. Then she looked at me and said simply, "Bad idea."

"Why?" I asked in confusion.

She lowered her head, scrunched up her face and said, "Because the Captain and the two security guards who checked everyone before we came onto the boat were the other three people in the room with Samir."

Oh. Yep, that was definitely a problem.

Chapter Six

"Okay, I am a bit confused now," Aly said. "We are, y'all, the 'Night Heroes.' Everybody goes to sleep, we wake up in the past, we deal with things that only we can deal with, we go to sleep, and we come home. But even though all of that is real, this is, well, 'realer.'"

"Ugghhhh! No, Sis, just no!" Carrie said as she squinted her eyes tightly shut and grabbed the side of her head as if having a migraine headache. "Terrorists or not, do NOT, ever, say 'realer.' I think I would rather go to a watery grave than have that abomination of grammatical expression bouncing around in my brain."

"You know what I mean, Carrie," Aly huffed, "even if I am bending your precious grammar rules a bit to say it. We have no

Conductor. We have not been 'called' to this. We are kids. And we are, and this is really important, ON VACATION. I don't want to fight terrorists; I want to snorkel and play putt-putt and eat stupid amounts of food. Why don't we pass this one off to someone else? How about mom and dad? They can handle pretty much anything, right?"

I actually thought about that for a few seconds, then shook my head.

"No, Sis. Yes, mom is brilliant, and dad is the strongest, toughest man I know. But if we put them on the trail, would we be able to just back off completely and let them handle it alone?"

"No," Carrie said emphatically. "We would, whether they liked it or not, trail them and get involved, and that would most assuredly blow our cover. When they saw us in action, we would have some pretty serious explaining to do. Besides, even as tough and smart as they are, could any of us live with ourselves if anything happened to them as a result of us getting them involved?"

We all fell silent at that. We knew we couldn't. This was, good idea or bad idea, up to us. We had to stop them, and we had to do so all while acting perfectly normal in front of mom and dad.

Just like always.

Impending doom or not, I insisted that Carrie take two or three trips down the waterslide before we sprang into action. If it were up to her, we would have started at once, but trying to think like mom and dad, I wanted to make sure she had some fun on this vacation as well.

But fifteen minutes later, we were heading for the room to get dried out. We had about three and a half hours until lunchtime when mom and dad would be expecting us to meet them for pizza.

Once we got dried off, cleaned up, and dressed, we sat down on the floor in a circle and tried to lay some plans out for what we would do.

"Okay, Sis," I said to Carrie, "give me every bit of information you can think of that will help us figure out what to do. Then, as always, we will pray and get to it."

"Well, to begin with, you should know that they have a very substantial advantage, namely that they will not be concerned with trying to escape with their own lives. They will almost certainly be planning on going down with the ship. That will make things a bit harder; people who don't care whether they live or die are much harder to deal with than rational, normal people."

Aly twisted up her face and cocked her head and looked over at Carrie like she could not comprehend what was being said, so Carrie pressed the explanation a bit farther.

"Martyrdom is a very big concept anong Islamic terrorists. They believe that dying in jihad is a surefire ticket to paradise for them. That is why the hijackers on 9/11 had no problem flying those planes into the buildings, knowing that they would be the first ones to die."

I let out a slow, head shaking whistle.

"Wow, that will make things more difficult. Everyone we have ever dealt with before did not mind harming or killing others, but they themselves always wanted to live. Dealing with people who actually want to die in the process of killing others will certainly complicate this. What else can you tell us?"

"Well," she said slowly, "since they will want to cause the most deaths possible and also get the greatest 'bang for the buck' publicity-wise, they will somehow want to record and/or broadcast it, which means it will likely happen during broad daylight. But in order to keep anyone from being close enough to be rescued, they will want to pick a spot in the ocean as far away from other vessels and potential rescuers as they can."

"Um, Sis," Aly said with the same scrunched up look on her face, "won't everyone just run to the lifeboats? That would sort of defeat their whole plan, don't you think?"

"Yes. Which means that if I were them, I would probably try to find a way to destroy or disable the lifeboats before the attack. We will need to pay attention to that."

"Okay," I said as the picture was forming in my mind, "then I would say the first thing we need to do is a full reconnaissance of this boat. We need to know everything that can be learned about it, every level, from front to back. And since this is not like a normal mission, meaning we have no idea if we have a full five days or not, the attack could come at any moment, so we need to do things as quickly as possible.

"We have just over three hours before lunch. As much as I hate to say it, we're going to need to split up."

The girls nodded at me, we each picked a few levels, with me taking the upper levels, Carrie the middle levels, and Aly the lower levels. We agreed to meet back in the room ten minutes before lunchtime so we could go meet mom and dad together, rather than arousing suspicion by arriving individually.

And then, official mission or not, we started the way every child of God ought to start when dealing with anything that is beyond them. Three Night Heroes suddenly embroiled in terror by day, bowed six knees, and brought three tender hearts before the King of kings.

"Lord, we are aware just how out of our element we are on this. But though we are out of our element, we are not out of yours. Not one thing has ever caught you by surprise, including this. Lord, three thousand souls are on this ship, including us, and including mom and dad. Please, Lord, help us to go where we need to go, see what we need to see, and do what we need to do. Give us understanding beyond our years and strength beyond our muscles. Grant us full success for the sake of everyone on board the ship and for Your great glory. We pray this in Jesus' name, Amen."

And then we were out the door, just three young vacationers somehow thrust in a position where everyone we passed would either live or die based on how well we did what we needed to do.

No pressure.

Chapter Seven

Pizza by the Sea is, first and foremost, pizza. This is to say that it is completely delicious. Whoever dreamed up the idea of rolling out soft dough and baking it up with tomato sauce, cheese, and all kinds of ingredients really deserves some kind of trophy or something.

But while pizza has the potential to bring most of humanity together, it also illustrates how very unique every one of us is.

Dad was munching on a supreme, too many ingredients to count, including nasty things like peppers and black olives. Mom had a much simpler white pizza with spinach, still nasty, but not quite as nasty as what dad had. Carrie was actually eating a calzone, which is sort of like a folded-up pizza. Aly had a simple cheese pizza, and I, apparently the only one with perfect taste, was devouring a meat lovers pizza.

"So," dad asked mom in between bites, "what did you think of the artwork in the gallery?"

Mom laughed a bit of a gentle laugh and replied, "I think it was mostly overpriced. That said, some of the Thomas Kincaid prints were pretty nice, and all of the Mark Keathly works were breathtaking."

Dad nodded in agreement, then turned to us.

"Did you guys enjoy the water slide?"

I smiled, both on the outside and on the inside. I was very glad at that moment I had convinced Carrie to take a few trips down it.

"Absolutely!" Aly said with enthusiasm. "You ought to try it!"

Dad grinned and quickly replied, "Oh, no worries there, I'm quite sure I will before the week is out."

We spent the next forty-five minutes happily and casually eating and talking, enjoying each other's company. All the while, though, I knew the girls and I were anxious to get somewhere quiet to talk for a while and discuss what we had all learned. But that was probably going to be a while…

"Okay, Warners," dad intentionally drawled, "what say we mosey out into the ship

46

and find something fun to do? Any suggestions?"

It was our family composition that made the choice. By that, I mean, when the girls outnumber the guys three to two, a lot of "girl things" tend to happen.

"A spa day? Seriously?" Dad asked, sort of skeptically.

"Don't worry, sweetheart," mom reassured, "while the girls and I are getting pampered, you and 'the man child' can be right next door at the gym if you like."

I was both relieved and thrilled. Gym time? Oh boy, do we like!

The next couple of hours were filled with metal and muscles. We bench pressed. We did dips. Dumbbell presses. By the time it was all said and done, we had done more exercises than I could count. I was sore, dad was sore, though he would never admit it, and we were both happy. I love spending time like that with my dad. I feel sort of sorry for boys who don't have that kind of relationship with their own dad.

It turned out to be pretty good timing as we walked out of the gym, we ran into the Warner ladies walking out of the spa at the exact same time. We happily meandered back toward the other side of the boat, down a couple of levels, and to our rooms. We spent the next little while showering off and cleaning up, resting, and reading.

Were our lives and the lives of everyone else at risk that very moment? Yes, yes, they were.

And yet somehow, I was as happy and peaceful as a baby held in his mother's arms.

I guess somehow it had not really occurred to us that we would be going back to the Star of the Sea for supper each night of the cruise.

We walked in, were once again pleasantly greeted by name, and shown to another table. And sure enough, once again, it was Sneaky Samir (as we Night Heroes had nicknamed him) that waited on our table. He was all smiles once again and spoke to us like we were his oldest and dearest friends.

I had the overwhelming urge to stand up and unload a right hook into his jaw. I did not do so for two reasons. One, that would have gotten us arrested and thrown off the boat, and therefore unable to save everyone else's lives. Two, I knew I could not handle him. I have fought some strong, dangerous, full-grown men. But no one so clearly as powerful and deadly as him. It occurred to me that if, as so often happens, this came down to a fight between him and me, I would very likely lose.

I would just have to count on the same God who has given us victory every time so far, giving me victory in that as well.

This night was something of an Italian feast in the Star of the Sea. We had more kinds of pasta than you can shake a stick at, all covered with delicious things like steak and chicken and shrimp. Of course, dad had to go and put a few nasty things on his; mussels, those little slug-like creatures inside of black shells. Who in the world eats things like that? He positively declares that they are delicious, but sixty-six percent of us Warner kids were unwilling to take the chance; only Carrie, naturally, would give them a try.

"Hmm. Your taste, dear father of mine, is impeccable, as usual," she said with dramatic stuffiness.

"Of course, it is, less diminutive female progeny," he answered equally stuffily.

"Puhleeeaaase, could you two talk, like, you know, 'normally?'" Aly whined.

"You mean, like, using, like, the word like, way too much?" he said with a mischievous grin.

"Okay, you two," mom intervened, "put your verbal swords back in their sheaths. Let's focus on what's important right now... dessert!"

"That's my mom!" Aly practically shouted, as folks from tables all around us looked over at her.

Mom giggled, dad dropped his head and shook it back and forth in pretend embarrassment, and Carrie and I just rolled our eyes.

But dessert put us all back on the same page pretty quickly. We had key lime pie, chocolate pie, and, well, lots of other pie.

Dad pushed the small plate with the last couple of bites still sitting on it away and groaned. "Yep, miserable again."

We all nodded in agreement, and then mom said, "Well, why don't we go to the open café on the upper deck and spread out on one of the big tables and play a game? Aly, I am assuming you brought the 'Bull' cards?"

"Oh yeah, momser, you know I did!"

Momser? All of us laughed at that. Aly was never disrespectful when she said things like that; she was just being her hyper, funny, lightning in a bottle self.

We made our way back to the room, grabbed the cards, and headed up to the Sea Bird café. For the next two hours, we played a hysterical game of Bull, which basically involved trying to fool people into thinking you either have cards that you do not have or do not have cards that you do have. We played, we shouted, and we laughed so hard that at times we could barely breathe.

And when everything was said and done, Dad, as usual, had won most of the games. I am telling you that man has a poker face like you would not believe. When he wants to be, he is utterly unreadable. I am convinced he could have the weight of the world on his shoulders and yet never show it.

Finally, we made our way back down to the rooms, crammed ourselves all into mom and dad's room for a few minutes, and prayed together as a family, just like we had done for every single day of my sixteen plus years.

And then we all hugged, told each other how much we loved them, and went our separate ways for the night.

And as soon as we closed our door behind us, the relaxation and good vibes were instantly gone.

"Okay, Night Hero girls, let's lay the important cards out on the table."

Chapter Eight

"Well," Carrie began, "The middle decks yielded nothing. Everything looks exactly like how I suspect it ought to look. Lots of locked rooms, plenty of restaurants, game rooms, the boring art gallery, blah blah blah, no sign of terrorism. What about you, little sister?"

"Mostly the same 'blah blah blah' as your middle decks, except fewer restaurants. But I can tell you that the two security guards that are apparently involved in all of this with the Captain and Samir are, quite literally, parked right in front of the stairs going down to the lower decks. I mean, they literally are sitting on chairs in front of them. The elevator only goes down to that level; in order to get any lower, as far as I can tell, you have to take those stairs."

"Well, that pretty much tells us where we need to go, doesn't it?" I said, shaking my head slowly. "And it makes perfect sense. Planting a bomb on the lower levels of the ship would ensure that no passenger accidentally wanders by and stumbles upon it. Furthermore, when it blows, the effect on the ship would be immediate and devastating. I suspect this puppy would go down in mere minutes.

"And that brings us to problem number two. My search of the upper decks confirmed our fears about all of the lifeboats. I casually but carefully checked them out, trying not to look suspicious. Three of them in a row have had the power wires to the lowering motors cut. I have no doubt in my mind that every single one of them is in the exact same condition. Those boats are going nowhere."

"In other words," Aly said seriously, "if we don't find and stop that bomb from going off, everybody on this boat will be sitting ducks."

"No, honey," Carrie replied with a wrinkled up brow, "ducks would be able to swim to safety."

"Ahh, yeah, bad analogy, I guess. So what do we do?"

"Well," I said slowly, "I would say we do the last thing we really want to do. I very much enjoyed sleeping on these peaceful waves last night. But I am guessing we should wait a while till we are pretty sure mom and dad are asleep, and then go 'Night Heroing.'"

"Agggh! Another one! That is as bad as Aly's 'realer'! Can we please not try to make a verb out of hero?"

Aly and I just rolled our eyes at her, then, since we had already prayed together as a family, we set our phones (which we had never had before; mom and dad got them for us just in time for the cruise, so we could stay in touch by text on the boat using the ship's wifi) for two o'clock in the morning, then laid down for a few hours of sleep before "going to work."

~~~~~~

Getting up at two in the morning is bad enough; getting up at two in the morning on an ocean liner, when you are supposed to be on vacation, is lots and lots worse.

"Ugggghhhh," Aly groaned when the alarms started chirping, "do we really have to get up? I was sleeping so good."

"Sleeping so -" Carrie began, but Aly stuck a stiff hand out and cut her off.

"No grammar Nazi at two in the morning!!!"

Carrie shrugged and started heading for the bathroom to get ready to go out and be a

55

hero. When she was done, I did so, and then Aly. After about twenty minutes, we were all awake and semi-alert, and it was time to plan and pray.

"Okay, this time, we all stay together. It will look a lot less suspicious for three kids to be wandering the boat together this time of morning than it will to be alone."

"Agreed, big brother," Carrie said simply. "But this is a big boat, so our wandering better not be exactly aimless. I would assume we will be making our way to the lower decks and looking for a way in, correct?"

"Definitely. Who knows, maybe we can find the bomb, get rid of it, go back to bed, and rest easy the rest of the night, and then wake up to enjoy the remainder of our vacation."

"Um, no!" Aly said, and I knew by her raised eyebrows and her sharp tone of voice that I had missed something.

"What, sis? Spit it out."

"If we just deal with the bomb, the bad guys will just make another one later and kill a bunch of other people. If we are going to go to the trouble of dealing with it, we also need to go ahead and deal with them."

Now that made sense. I didn't particularly like it, but it made sense.

"Okay, then. We deal with the bomb, and then somehow deal with the bombers. With that big of a task ahead of us, we better not just pray, we better pray hard."

And we did; three vacationing Night Heroes, wishing we could just have fun but knowing that responsibility must always come first, especially when lives were on the line.

Chapter Nine

A cruise ship at night is very different from a cruise ship during the day. There were still people everywhere, but nowhere near the amount that was there earlier in the day when the sun was in the sky. And those that were out and about, fortunately, seemed to be tied up in the their own thoughts and doings and in no way seemed concerned about three kids doing their own thing.

As we made our way toward the center of the ship and the elevators, we planned on taking down to the lower levels, we tossed around ideas as to how we could get past the two guards we knew would be stationed down there and waiting.

"Surely, they can't be down there twenty-four hours a day," Aly said. "I mean, they have to sleep sometime, right?"

"I rather suspect," Carrie said with a pensive glance toward her, "that one of them will be taking the night shift, as it were, or that they will have more people involved in this plot than just the four that we know of."

When we got to the center of the ship, it was even more breathtaking at night than it was during the day. We could look straight up through the giant skylight and see the lovely stars up above us, and the moonlight gleaming down through it as well, shedding light far more breathtaking than any of the neon fixtures it was overshadowing in the midst of all of the shops and people.

"We serve a pretty amazing God," Carrie whispered, and Aly and I just nodded in agreement.

"It's a shame everyone doesn't serve that same God, isn't it?' Aly asked a bit sadly. "Especially when they choose to serve other gods, false gods, really, who expect them to kill themselves in the process of killing others, and not for any good reason whatsoever. It seems weird to think they could look at all of this beauty and somehow still get the idea that a good God would want to have anything to do with bloodshed like that."

"I don't know, Sis. But from what I've heard dad teach and preach, these folks with a jihad mentality have been raised in this belief system, not just for their entire lives, but for generation after generation before them as well. If that is all you have ever known, I guess it would be that much harder to ever really see and appreciate the truth."

"Don't make me feel sorry for them, Kyle, I will have a much harder time gnawing their legs off up to their kneecaps if you do."

Carrie and I just laughed at that. One thing I definitely didn't want to do was dull the edge of my fireball little sister right now. I suspected that before this adventure was over, we were going to need every little bit of that fire and every ounce of that edge.

"So, what's our play, big brother?" Carrie asked. "How are we going to approach the guard point?"

I thought about that for a minute, and then said, "Well, like we heard R.B. Oullette preach once from Acts 27:44, why don't we 'use what we have?' We are kids going up against adults. So why don't we use what could be a weakness as a strength instead?"

I could see the questioning looks on Carrie and Aly's faces, so I pressed the explanation a bit further.

"Aly, how good of a puppy dog face can you get? I mean, like the thing you do at Christmas time when you really, really want dad to get you some particular thing?"

"Christmas time? You mean like, 'all the time'?" Carrie said with a smirk.

"Har har, Sis, very funny. And yes, Kyle, if you are suggesting that I play 'innocent smiling kid' and melt the heart of Mr. Terrorist with my big eyes, I can do that. It won't be quite as much fun as the Vaseline, sparklers, and tabasco, which I did not bother to bring anyway since we are on vacation, but I suppose it will do."

"You know, Sis, you have been talking about that ever since our first adventure. One of these days, whatever it is, you are going to have to break it out for us!"

She just smirked and said, "Oh, you know it!"

Then we all made our way to the elevator and headed down to the floor above where we needed to be. It was time to get into action; lives were on the line.

When the door opened, Carrie turned to Aly, hugged her, and said, "Be careful, little sister, this isn't a game."

Aly nodded to Carrie and winked at me, and we then stepped off the elevator. As the door closed with her still in the elevator, I quickly and silently said one more prayer to my heavenly Father, a prayer that He would protect my precious little sister. That runt and I fought like cats and dogs most of the time, but the thought of anyone else hurting her wasn't even something I could begin to fathom. I would kill or die before I would let that happen.

Hey, this is Aly, I will pick the story up from here.

The doors to the elevator closed with an ominous finality, separating me from my brother and sister, the rest of the team, apart from mom and dad, my biggest heroes.

You know, thinking about it, I played brave most of the time, and I suppose I am sort of brave, given all we have been through, but to be honest, I was a little bit nervous. I never did particularly like it when we had to split up; I knew there was safety in numbers. Dad taught us that from the Bible since the time we were little. I began to hastily quote the verses in my mind as the elevator began its descent. Ecclesiastes 4:12 "And if one prevail against him, two shall withstand him; and a threefold cord is not quickly broken." Kyle and Carrie and I had, through eight missions thus far, become that threefold cord. We had survived through things most kids could never even dream of.

I was really missing my other two cords at that moment.

But I also knew that my real strength was from my Heavenly Father and that He was with me even when no one else could be. As the elevator sank, my hopes raised based on that thought.

When the doors opened, though, those hopes gulped and panicked just a bit, as I got a rather unexpected shock.

"Hello, Aly Warner. What brings you down to this level?"

It was the captain!

Drat! He knew my name, too! Did all these bad guys have a photographic memory?

Quickly recovering my wits, I said, "Oh, hello, Mr. Captain, what brings you off the bridge down to this level?" That was good; it seemed to throw him off stride just a little bit. But only for a second.

"Oh, well, as Captain, I am responsible for every square floating inch of this ship, so you are likely to see me anywhere. Now again, what brings you down here? There isn't any food or any games down here, or anything to interest anyone of your age, especially this time of the morning."

Drat. Now I was on the defensive. But only for a split second. After all we Night Heroes have been through, I was pretty confident that I could match wits with the best of them.

"Oh, well, my brother and sister and I are actually playing an epic game of hide-and-seek. I have gone over the upper levels pretty thoroughly, so I thought maybe they came down here to the lower levels. I don't exactly want to cheat or anything, but I don't suppose you have seen them down here, have you? If you have, I promise not to rat you out for telling me!"

I gave him my most mischievous grin, and he returned it with a smile of his own, a smile that looked playful and friendly, although I knew that the devil himself was behind it.

"No, I have not seen them. But if I had, you can be most sure that I would tell you straightaway. Now, why don't you run along back up to the higher levels? No one is allowed down here save for the crew. It's, well, not safe to be down here with all of the dangerous equipment and everything else we have, and I simply could not bear the thought of any precious child such as yourself being hurt in any way."

I bet, I thought to myself as I smiled on the outside while inwardly screaming *Liar!* at him and kicking him in the shin. But I didn't let that thought show on my face. I just said, "Yes, Sir, Mr. Captain, or should I say, Aye aye, sir!"

He smiled, I smiled, and then I turned and made my way back into the elevator. I pressed the button that would close the door, separating me from this wolf in captain's clothing, and carry me back up one floor to rejoin Carrie and Kyle. Boy, they were not going to like this!

Chapter Ten

When the doors opened and I stepped off the elevator to meet Kyle and Carrie, I guess they could tell by the look on my face that things had not gone well.

"What?" Carrie said simply.

"You aren't going to believe this..."

When I told them that it was the Captain himself guarding the entrance to the lower levels, Kyle just shook his head and let out a low, slow whistle, then said, "They really aren't taking any chances, are they? The good news in all of this, I suppose, is that there probably aren't any more than four involved in the plot. If there were, I doubt seriously if the Captain himself would be taking a shift guarding the lower levels."

"Well, that bit of good news notwithstanding," Carrie said, "what in the world are we going to do now? Apparently, even in the middle of the night, we aren't going to be able to get down there."

"I don't know, Sis, I just don't know," Kyle said, and he sounded both worried and thoughtful as he said it. "For now, let's head back to bed and take the Daniel and company route."

Carrie and I nodded out heads; we knew exactly what he meant. In Daniel chapter two, Daniel, Shadrach, Meshach, and Abednego were about to be killed, them and all the wise men of Babylon, simply because king Nebuchadnezzar could not remember a dream. Yes, that is pretty drastic. But Nebuchadnezzar was, and here is a big word that Carrie taught me, "autocratic." That means that he had absolute power. His word was literally law in Babylon the second he spoke it. He did not have to obey the law; he was the law.

So Daniel and his three friends, realizing the danger they were in (just like we three Night Heroes and thousands of unsuspecting passengers aboard ship with us at that moment) went to their rooms and went to prayer. And in the middle of the night, God gave them exactly what they needed by way of information in a dream. Daniel and everyone else was saved, and we would just have to count on God doing the same thing for us.

Chapter Eleven

"GOOD MORNING, GOOD MORNING, GOOD MORNING, GOOD MORNING, GOOD MORNING, TO YOU!!!

"GOOD MORNING, GOOD MORNING, GOOD MORNING, GOOD MORNING, GOOD MORNING, TO YOOOOOOOOOUUUUUUU!!!"

Hey, this is Kyle, I will pick up the story from here. My reaction to the above, loud, VERY loud song? Ugggh. It was him again, Dad, Mr. Chipper. Whenever we Warner kids are sleepy or sluggish in the morning, since the time we were very little, he had the habit of bursting into our rooms and singing that song at the top of his voluminous lungs.

All three of us just sort of groaned and pulled the pillows up over our heads.

"What is wrong with you sleepy heads?" we heard mom ask. Apparently, she had come in right behind him during his little "morning cheerfulness prank."

"We didn't sleep too well last night," Carrie said truthfully.

"Seriously?" dad asked. "How can anyone not sleep well in a ship out on the ocean with the waves rocking you gently like a baby in the Savior's arms?"

Oh, dad, if only you knew!

Tired or not, we were pretty quickly up, awake, and ready. Yes, breakfast was calling our names, but it was much more than that as well. Today would be a shore excursion! There is an island that the ship would be docking near, an island actually owned by the cruise line. We would get to go ashore and snorkel all day, play in the water, eat island food, relax, just the best of the best kind of a day.

Suddenly, the best part of that equation hit me. We would not be in any danger for most of this day. It would not accomplish much for the cause of jihad for them to blow the ship up in shallow water just off the coast of an island with most everyone safely ashore. Secure in that knowledge, I felt pretty light and happy as we Warners made our way to breakfast together one more time.

How many more times we would get to do that simple thing I just did not know. It mostly depended on how successful we were at doing the things that nobody but God knew we were doing.

Breakfast was delicious. Again. How was I ever going to go back to cereal and milk after all of this cruise food?

We all ate sort of light at this breakfast, though, knowing we would want to save a bunch of room for the island food we would be getting at lunch. Once we were done with breakfast, we made our way back to the room and gathered our things for the shore excursion. We had all made sure to bring along our own snorkels. Something I always feel sort of icky about when I thought of renting them was the realization that I had no idea where they had been, or how well they had been cleaned. I guess I get that from my dad, Mr. Germophobia.

Going for a shore excursion on a cruise is a pretty cool experience. There are smaller boats, ferry style, that stay docked at the island all the time. When you go on a shore excursion, those smaller boats will make their way out to the ship, one after the other, carrying people to the shore about a hundred at a time. The ferry boat obviously felt a lot different than the ocean liner, but it was still amazingly cool. I suppose there is nothing I like better than the ocean; it just seems to be one more cool, blue reminder of the glory and goodness of my God, almost like a gigantic swimming pool that He made just for us, simply because He loves us.

The trip from the boat to the shore only took about five minutes. The ship could only have been about a half mile offshore or so. Once the ferry was docked, everyone disembarked and headed for the beach to find a place they could call their own for the day, or they went to the pavilion area.

None of us kids even had asked our dad where we would be going or what we would be doing for the day. If dad was ever anywhere near crystal clear ocean water, we knew he would be out in it.

We made our way to the beach, and to no one's surprise, mom had brought a book and quickly had an umbrella set up. I knew she was not much of a person for getting out in the water. But give her some rest time, which she never seemed to get much of, some sand, some sunshine, and an umbrella for shade, and she would crack open a book and be happy and peaceful for hours.

Dad, not so much. Oh, he is a reader, too, a voracious reader. But he never ever passes up the opportunity to go snorkeling. Nor do any of his adventurous kids. Within just a few minute's time, we were all casually and happily paddling out away from the crowd and over the reefs.

The reefs of a tropical island are always an amazing thing, and to me, just more evidence of our glorious Creator. If you have ever snorkeled over a lovely school of neon-colored fish, you won't have any trouble believing that "In the beginning, God created the heaven and the earth."

There were blue ones with funny shaped faces, red ones that looked like someone had given them tiny wings, and yellow ones that, for some reason, made me think of a bunch of schoolteachers. And I have no idea why on that last one.

There were fish with long snouts that made it look like someone had stretched out their faces and crossed them with an anteater. There was even the occasional little octopus huddled in a hole of the reef somewhere looking out at us with wild eyes as if to say, "Don't come any nearer, odd-looking quadruped!"

As beautiful as all of the fish were, I knew that dad would be in hunting mode. He had almost a supernatural ability to go snorkeling and find the most amazing things to bring home with him. I knew before the day was out that he would find conch shells, ocean snail shells, starfish, and much more.

Carrie was almost just as good as him at that and just as natural in the water. I was pretty good at all of that myself, and Aly was coming along nicely, too.

In the midst of the snorkeling and happiness, I could feel a bit of anger creeping into my heart. As I was swimming along, from time to time, I would go over the top of something that never should have been there; trash. Bottles, cans, other things like that. I tell you, that makes my blood boil every single time! Our God made this world, how dare anyone trash it up like that. Christians especially ought to take care of this world better than anyone else, knowing that it was given to us as a gift from our God.

But the moment of anger quickly passed, as off to my right I caught sight of a sand dollar. It was in about ten feet of water. So I took a big gulp, held my breath, and dove down for the bottom. I had no trouble reaching it, and I carefully picked it up off the bottom to avoid breaking it. I pushed off and came back to the top, blew out very hard to clear the snorkel, then lowered my mask so I could clearly see my treasure.

It was absolutely beautiful and big enough to cover my entire palm.

"That's a nice one, Sport," dad said from behind me. I whirled to look over my shoulder and see him; I had not known he was there. I smiled at him, both because of the compliment, and the realization that he always seemed to be there to watch over us kids.

We all snorkeled happily for the next couple of hours, and then made our way to the beach and laid our treasures out.

Sure enough, dad had brought in quite a haul of beautiful shells. But all the rest of us had done pretty well also. My palm-sized sand dollar, I think, was the nicest one of them all. There was one odd item, as dad noted.

"A rock, son? It is pretty, but don't we have plenty enough of those back home?"

I just smiled innocently and said, "Yes, sir, but we don't have any from the Bahamas."

We laid everything out on a towel in the sun to dry, including ourselves. Under the Bahamian sun, it doesn't take long to get dry and warm.

Chapter Twelve

"DING DING DING!" came the sound of a bell from the pavilion, and all of us quickly got up and started heading that way, recognizing it as the sound of the dinner bell. It was letting everyone know that the delicious food was ready.

This would be an amazing lunch, nothing even remotely fast food-ish or even American-ish. I am not opposed to fast food or American food obviously, but if a person travels to a foreign land, they are sort of crazy not to take advantage of the opportunity to eat things that they will never be able to get back home.

There was flying fish, curry chicken, an odd kind of beans and rice that can only be gotten down there in that part of the world, and all of it was spiced to perfection. There was also an amazing island punch made with the fresh fruits found right there on those islands; mangoes, guavas, and other things that do not grow readily in America.

We went back for seconds, and for thirds, and were pretty quickly stuffed and happy.

"What say we make our way out to the beach and rest for a little while," mom said, and all of us happily agreed. After a meal like that, and with the toasty warm sun still shining down, a rest under God's sunshine would be a beautiful thing.

And rest we did.

We whiled away the next couple of hours, variously reading, napping, staring out at the waves, and in general, just having the most relaxing time of our lives.

But as the sun got nearer and nearer to the horizon, my thoughts began to turn toward the ship anchored just a half-mile offshore. She looked so peaceful anchored there on the placid sea. And yet seven people knew better: the four terrorist conspirators determined to bring her down, and the three Night Heroes determined to stop them.

After resting for a while, we played some volleyball on the beach. In fact, it was team Warner, all five of us, against five other random people from the ship that had put together an impromptu team. I hate to brag, but we absolutely blew them apart. And the best of the best of us was also the smallest—Aly. That girl loves volleyball as much as I love basketball, and she is really, really good at it. Her serves are perfect and powerful, and she is an amazing setter, which made dad and I both very happy. She made us look good as we got spike after spike from her perfect sets just in front of the net.

We dispatched our opponents, shook their hands and smiled, and then heard the horn sound letting us know it was time to make our way back to the ferry boats and back to the ship.

We wandered back to the beach, made sure we gathered all of our stuff, including our newfound treasures, and made our way to the ferry. Everything had been absolutely wonderful, and all of us were as happy and peaceful as we could be.

Now, if we could just deal with some terrorists and their bomb, maybe we could enjoy the rest of our vacation this way as well. Although, the thought occurred to me that that was probably not the case since one of those terrorists just so happened to be the captain. If we did stop them, who in the world would run the ship? Weird thoughts that you get when you are thinking of things this out of the ordinary...

Once we got back to the ship, we had about an hour to get cleaned up before supper, and that gave Carrie and Aly and me time to talk in our room.

"Well, did you get an answer during the night?" Aly asked, looking back and forth between Carrie and me.

I smiled.

"I do believe I did, Sis, and if I may say so, I believe you especially are going to like it."

"Distraction?" She asked with an excited look on her face.

Carrie immediately looked horrified at the suggestion.

"Oh no, you can't be blowing anything up here. This isn't Charleston, and it isn't 1858."

I just smiled at her and said, "No worries, my overly concerned sister. Yes, distraction. But no to the explosion part."

"And exactly what kind of a distraction do you believe that you can put together that will get all of our four conspirator's attention away from the lower level?" Carrie asked.

"Well," I responded, "obviously we have to be a little more careful than normal. We can't do anything like an actual fire, since fire is the most dangerous thing on any ship anywhere, and we ourselves could be the cause of thousands of deaths. But we also cannot do anything small and silly like pulling a fire alarm, because that would be too easily and quickly dealt with.

"But there is one disaster that is absolutely, positively guaranteed to get everyone's attention; I mean all hands on deck — man overboard."

"Oh no, big brother, I am not jumping off this ship just to stop it from going down!" Aly said as she stomped her foot.

"Whoa, whoa, whoa, Sis, easy there. We are not putting you at risk like that. And risk is a bit too mild of a word. First of all, hitting the water from this high up would be about the same as hitting a concrete parking lot; you would not likely even survive the impact. Secondly, anyone actually going overboard on a ship, especially at night, is pretty much dead even if they do somehow survive the fall. It takes the ship too long to get back around to where they were to even begin to rescue them, even if they were able to find them, which in and of itself is almost impossible.

"Long story short, most people that fall overboard have no chance of even surviving.

"I'm not talking about actually sending anybody overboard; I'm talking about making a big splash, and then simply shouting man overboard. That will demand everyone's full attention, there will have to be a full accounting of every passenger to find out who, if anyone, is gone. And while that accounting is happening, the ship itself will have to be swinging back around. That normally takes, if I have heard correctly, about two full hours.

"That should give us the time to get down to the lower level and somehow deal with that bomb."

"Well, what are we going to do when they find out that no one actually went overboard?" Aly asked, with her hands thrown up in exasperation.

"Does that really matter?" I asked. "We will have done the job of saving everyone's life."

"But what about actually dealing with the terrorists? How are we going to keep them from trying to do it again, even if we stop them this time?" Carrie asked.

"Well, about the best I have been able to figure out on that is that once we find the bomb, before we deal with it, we take pictures of it and text those pictures to the authorities on the mainland."

"And what in the world is to keep them from thinking that we are the terrorists?!?" Carrie practically shrieked. "Do you want to get us sent to prison forever?"

Frustrated by their lack of help, I shot back, "Well, I don't hear either of the two of you coming up with anything better! So now is your chance; speak now or forever hold your peace. Or at least hold it till the bomb blows up, and the ship goes down."

They both got completely silent.

Four or five seconds later, Carrie finally said, "For the record, as your plans go, this is one of the dumbest ones ever. But, since I can't seem to think of anything better, I guess we go and do it your way. But it's still a dumb idea."

"Um, excuse me, brilliant older sister and strong older brother, isn't there a glaring oversight in this already dumb plan?"

"And what would that be, pipsqueak?" I asked.

"You keep using the term 'Deal with the bomb.' How exactly do you intend to deal with a bomb? Do you have any idea how to defuse a bomb? Or are you just going to start ripping out wires and hope that you don't end up being the one that blows us all up?"

My jaw dropped open. I had not thought of that. At all.

"I think I have the answer to that one," Carrie said with a smile. "We are in the middle of the ocean. A bomb going off in the ocean won't be a bit of trouble. We don't have to defuse the bomb; we just have to get it overboard. Surely between the three of us, we can carry it up to the deck and dump it. We just have to make sure that no one sees us or tries to stop us as we do so."

Aly grimaced and slapped her forehead four or five times with her palm as she said, "This is a terrible plan, a terrible plan, a terrible plan. I cannot believe I'm going to go along with this!"

I put both my hands on her shoulders. "I know, pipsqueak, I know. But unless we can come up with something better, we have to go with this. Tell you what. For now, let's just get cleaned up and get ready for supper; mom and dad should be knocking on our door at any minute. We'll pray as we eat. If we come up with something better while we eat, fine. But if not, sometime tonight we go into action. Agreed?"

"Agreed, Kyle. I may not particularly like it, but you can count on me."

And I knew that I could.

Chapter Thirteen

I very rarely get upset with my dad. This was one of those rarelys.

"Seriously?" I asked mom as we four Warners, minus dad, sat down at our table in The Star of the Sea. "He can't even go a few days without working on something ministry-related? I thought this was supposed to be a family vacation, a time of rest, a time to unwind? He has been telling us how important it is to relax from time to time."

"Kyle, you need to understand that sometimes a preacher has to do what he has to do. Souls are often very literally on the line, and if God is speaking to him, he dare not delay doing as he is told. Your dad has something very important to do, and he needs to do it right now. Cut him a little slack; sometimes, it isn't easy following the Lord, but your dad is always faithful to follow no matter what."

I calmed down and nodded my head at that. I knew she was right. If dad was missing supper to do some work, even on vacation, he had a good reason for it, and the Lord had a good reason for calling him to it.

"Besides," mom said, "he will surely join us for some game time after supper."

Supper was good and mostly consisted of what was called a Mediterranean feast. The main meat was lamb, which is something Americans don't get to eat very often. And boy, is that a shame! That stuff was delicious! Along with that, there were amazing salads with Mediterranean vegetables, many more hors d'oeuvres (which, much to my mother's chagrin I normally pronounced as "horse doovers" just for fun, even though it is really pronounced "or dervz") and all of it topped off, of course, by a delicious assortment of desserts. Once again, the food on the ship did not disappoint, and all four of us Warners were stuffed.

"Could I possibly get another cup of coffee?" Mom asked pleasantly to our waiter; this time, it was not Sneaky Samir. Carrie whispered to me when mom wasn't watching, "I bet Samir is 'busy' on guard right now."

Aly also got a cup of coffee, and the two of them sat there, slowly sipping and enjoying it. Carrie and I would rather have been out and about doing whatever, but since mom and Aly didn't seem to be in a hurry, we both got some punch and sat there sipping along with them.

"May I get you anything else?" The waiter asked as he passed by our table once more.

"Yes, please," mom asked, pleasantly, "I think I would like one more cup of coffee."

"Wow, seriously? How much coffee do adults drink, exactly?"

Mom just grinned, took another sip, and did not answer. I shook my head and vowed never to grow up if I was going to end up consuming that much of that black, tar-like substance.

After what seemed like an eternity filled with coffee, I saw dad making his way through the restaurant toward our table. He smiled at us, finished the trek there, leaned over and kissed mom, and sat down beside her.

"Sorry I had to let you folks do supper alone," he said, "I do apologize."

"Would you like anything to eat, honey?" Mom asked with an adoring smile.

"No, babe, that is fine, I am still not in the least bit hungry, lunch is still holding me over just fine. So, what would you guys like to do? If you have any suggestions, throw them out at me. But just know that I have my own suggestion…

The grin on his face as he said that made us perk up.

"Okay, spill it, dad, whatcha got?" Aly grinned.

"Well," he said, "it just so happens that there is actually a movie theater on this boat. And there is this movie playing that you may have heard of before, *The Incredibles*…"

Oh boy, that is all Aly needed to hear. Yes, the movie has been out for a while, but she cannot get enough of it. Somehow, I get the feeling that she sees our family in that family.

Since there was no objection from anyone, we made our way from the restaurant back to the middle of the ship, down one level, and over toward the movie theater. We quickly found some seats near the front and settled in for a relaxing time watching the movie. It was odd, though, seeing all those explosions, and realizing that we ourselves could be very near to a real one!

During the movie, I took the time to whisper back and forth to the girls. I wanted to know if either of them had come up with any better plan than mine or any refinements to mine. Long story short, the answer to those questions were no and no. So, it looked like sometime shortly after the movie was over, we were going to cause quite the scene on this boat.

I worried what mom and dad would think about all of this, but seeing as how we were trying to save both of their lives too, I put that thought aside.

After the final credits, we Warners moseyed out of the movie theater, and dad stretched a big stretch and yawned a big yawn.

"I am so tired!" He said. "What say tonight we all turn in just a little bit early and try to get some rest?"

I was absolutely thrilled with that idea, though I didn't want to let on too much.

"Yep, I suppose I am good with that since we didn't sleep too well last night," I said with a yawn of my own, and Aly and Carrie nodded their heads in agreement. I knew we Night Heroes were all thinking the same thing: time to get to work.

Once we got back to the rooms, we once again gathered in mom and dad's room, prayed together as a family, and then went our separate ways. I knew we would wait just a little while until we were fairly sure mom and dad would be asleep and then slip out and do what needed to be done.

I just prayed we would be successful.

Chapter Fourteen

Trash bags: check. Water from the shower to fill those trash bags: check. We could thank mom for those trash bags; it was her wise foresight for us to bring them along to keep our wet clothes in them. Little had we known that would be using them to make a "body" to throw overboard.

We got two or three of the trash bags filled, then took a dark sheet off the bed, laid the bags in it, and tied it up. We now had our "unfortunate victim."

"Okay, here's how we play this," I said. "Aly, you go up to the top deck. Make sure you are just above us. Carrie and I will drag the body out onto the balcony. When you get up there, give us a bird whistle to let us know that you are in place and ready. We will whistle back. Then we will dump the body, and as soon as you hear it hit the water, you start to point and scream that you saw somebody go overboard.

"As soon as you do, you can bet that within seconds, pandemonium is going to break loose on this boat. When it does, race for the elevators, and come down to this floor. We will meet you there and head down to the lower levels together."

"What if they leave a guard there waiting for us?"

"If they do, littlest sister, we will just have to be prepared to deal with him."

"Deal with him? Exactly how do you intend to do that, especially if it is Samir?"

I reached into the bag with my treasures that I had gotten snorkeling from earlier in the day and retrieved the rock. Then I picked up a long sock out of my suitcase, dropped the rock into the bottom of it, and said, "I think this will do the trick."

She just grinned in admiration and said, "Wicked, big brother, absolutely wicked!"

"Okay, let's do this."

Without a word, we knelt down together to pray one more time.

"Lord," I said, "We sure do need your help again. You have used us to save individuals, but now we simple kids find ourselves in a position where three thousand lives are in our hands. That scares me, to be honest. Lord, would you please help us not to mess up? Please let the distraction work like we need it to, let us be able to find that bomb, and let us be able to get rid of it. We ask all of this in Jesus' name, amen."

We got up from our knees, looked into each other's eyes, and Carrie said, "Let's do this."

Hey, this is Aly again. I headed out of the room and made my way toward the elevator. I was nervous, but for the weirdest reasons. We were about to disrupt the vacation of three thousand people by making this ship come to a stop and do a U-turn in the middle of the ocean. And then, if all of this didn't pan out, we were going to have to explain why we disrupted everyone's vacation. I was about to either have a whole lot of people mad at me or a whole lot of people dead.

Neither of those options seemed to be too incredibly great.

I just hoped the plan would work and that we could explain to everybody why we did what we did.

The elevator did not take long to get me up to the top deck. I took a deep breath, walked out on the deck, and made my way over to the railing of the ship to where I was pretty sure I was over the top of our room just a few decks down.

I gave my standard bird whistle… a few seconds of silence… and I heard Kyle whistle back. Good, I thought, I was in nearly perfect position. I waited and watched… Come on, guys… Come on, you can do this. Then my eyes caught a dark shadow going over the edge of the balcony, and about two seconds later, I heard a massive splash. A couple of other people nearby turned that direction, and I knew they had heard it too.

Instantly, I pointed down to the water and begin to scream at the top of my lungs, "Man overboard! Man overboard! I just saw somebody go overboard! Somebody get the captain! Somebody just went overboard!"

People begin to rush to the edge, and I heard a couple of people call, "We heard it too; we heard them splash in the water!"

Boy, oh boy, was Kyle right when he said it was about to be pandemonium!

Crew members started rushing for the deck, and within ten or fifteen seconds, I could feel the engines beginning to change. I knew the ship would have to make a large sweep to try to come back around to that spot, and that is what would give us our window of time to try and find and dispose of the bomb.

As the crowd began to get thicker and thicker at the deck edge, I began to push back through them, made my way back into the ship, and rushed for the elevator toward the front part of the ship, the elevator I knew Kyle and Carrie would be waiting at. We did not want to use the glass one in the middle of the ship, we did not want to risk being seen. I began to pound the buttons and was practically dancing in frustration that nothing was moving as fast as I needed it to.

"Come on, you stupid elevator come on!"

Finally, the doors opened. I jumped inside, slammed the "door close" button, and punched in the number for our floor. Everything seemed like it was moving in slow motion, though I knew with my brain that it was going just exactly as fast as always.

When it finally stopped and the doors opened, Kyle and Carrie practically shot inside.

"Close the door, close the door, take us down!" Kyle hissed.

"I'm on it, bro, I'm on it."

I slammed the right buttons, the door closed, and we were heading down to the bottom of the ship. I saw Kyle's "rock sock" in his hand. If anybody was standing in the way when we got we were going, they were going to end up with a massive headache.

Hey, this is Kyle, I will pick it up from here. We took that elevator down to one floor above where we needed to be, rushed out of it, and then back to the elevator in the middle of the ship. That one was, blessedly, right there on that level waiting for us somehow. We punched the buttons, danced as the interminably slow doors creaked open, and rushed inside. Down one more floor, and the doors opened yet again.

We rushed out with me in the lead, ready to sling that sock rock if needed.

But no one was there. We went down that previously carefully guarded flight of stairs like we were flying down a greased sliding board. We hit the door at the bottom of it… and stopped dead.

I reached for the handle, and it would not budge.

"It's locked!" Carrie shouted. "How could we have been so stupid! There is no way in the world they would leave this door unlocked if they were having to suddenly leave it unguarded."

"Stand back," I shouted, and the girls pretty quickly figured out what I had in mind. There was one square pane of glass on that door, one chance to gain entry. I knew that glass would be tempered, meaning really, really hard to break.

I begin to swing that rock in the sock around my head faster and faster and faster until it was whirling like a helicopter blade, then slammed it into that glass pane.

It shattered into a million pieces, and so did the rock.

No matter, it wasn't the rock that I was interested in any way. I had just picked it up to use as a weapon if needed.

I stuck my arm through the now broken glass pane, grabbed the handle from the inside and opened the door. We now had access; now, we just had to find and deal with that bomb.

Chapter Fifteen

The bowels of a cruise ship, the engine room and all the other rooms associated with it, don't look anything like a cruise ship. No linens, no carpet, no fancy napkins, no waiters in tuxedos; just tons of metal, pipes running everywhere, gauges, and small metal doors, it was an absolute labyrinth.

"Carrie, talk to me. What would be the most likely point for them to place the bomb to do the greatest amount of damage?"

"I am guessing toward the back of the boat, but not quite as far back as the engines themselves. They would want the blast to disable the engines, but to be far enough forward to allow the ship to be completely and quickly flooded."

Both Aly and I knew that Carrie was very rarely wrong in any of her guesses; her genius brain by now would have worked out all of the physics involved in this equation.

Without any debate, we all started running back that direction.

All along the way, there was room after room and compartment after compartment that we burst into. We found, well, "stuff," things that we had no idea what they were, but any shipman would quickly know, but nothing that looked anything like a bomb.

"Come on guys, be quick, keep going, we have to find this thing."

The sound of our tennis-shoed feet thudded softly but quickly as we continued to race toward the back of the ship, checking every compartment along the way. I knew we would not have forever, and I was beginning to feel the panic rising in my throat as area after area yielded nothing.

"We only have two or three more rooms before we hit the engine room, Kyle, come on!" Carrie shouted.

"I know," I shot back, "you and Aly take those two on the left, I will take the ones on the right. Hurry!"

We each ran for our targets and burst through our opposing doors at about the exact same time.

I screamed, "Nothing here!"

Carrie screamed, "Nothing here either!"

Aly just screamed. A bloodcurdling, terrifying scream.

Within seconds Carrie and I had rushed to her. It did not take us long to find out why she had screamed.

"Hello, Warner children," Samir said with a pleasantness that did not match the evil look on his face. He was holding the point of a knife, a long, brutal-looking knife, right at Aly's throat as she stood there frozen in front of him, utterly unmoving.

I had not seen a knife that deadly looking since the blade of Black Crow. And behind Samir, Aly, and the knife was a very large, deadly looking bomb.

"Hello yourself, Samir," I said with more composure than I actually felt. "Are jihadists such as yourself really so cowardly as to hold a knife to the throat of little girls?"

I knew Aly would not like that "little girl," comment, but I also knew she would understand what I was trying to do.

"You do have a much more suitable opponent here, why don't you let her go and try me instead? I think I will be much more of a match for you than you realize."

Samir just laughed an evil, dirty sounding laugh.

"Boy infidel," he spat, "I will gladly take you up on your offer and will even be so kind as to put the knife aside as I do. I will gladly cut the throat of your filthy sisters when I am done with you, but I have time for a bit of fun first."

He sheathed his knife, then in two quick, smooth movements backhanded Aly and then jabbed a straight punch into Carrie's face. Both of my sisters went down with a cry, and my blood was instantly boiling. Nobody, nobody, NOBODY does that to my sisters!

He grinned, spat, and motioned with both of his hands for me to come to him as he stepped a few feet away from where Carrie and Aly were lying on the ground unconscious so as to give us room.

I put my hands up and begin to circle warily. I was coldly, furiously angry. And yet as big and strong as I am for my age, I knew that I was so overmatched in size and strength that it would take a miracle for me to win this.

Samir feinted a jab, and I jerked a bit.

He laughed. "What's wrong, infidel, too much time playing video games to know how to fight?"

As he said that he spread his arms a bit to gesture. And I made him pay for that cockiness.

"Whap!" went my left jab as it made solid contact with his mouth. His head rocked just a bit... and he just stood there and smiled. Blood from his split lower lip stained his white teeth as he did. He licked his lip and teeth slowly, then said, "Ahhh, so the Jesus boy knows how to throw a punch! That is good, very good, it will make this much more enjoyable."

And then all hades broke loose on me.

Samir threw his own jab, straight, fast, and strong. I dipped my head to the left, and the blow glanced off the side of my head. Instantly he followed up with a compact right hook. And though I got both hands in front of it, it was so powerful that it knocked me backward.

I dropped my right leg back to catch my balance and steady myself, but no sooner had I done so than Samir whirled around with a spinning hook kick. I knew that if that made contact, I was done for.

I ducked under it. His foot hit the ground, and I lunged at him, and immediately ran into another lightning-fast straight left jab. My head rocked back, I tasted blood, and I knew I was in trouble. I raised both hands to defend my head and immediately felt all the air

103

leave my body as Samir caught me square in the stomach with a right.

As I doubled over, I knew what was coming. And when the uppercut hit me, lights flashed in my brain, my entire world went black, and as I fell, I knew that we were all going to die.

Chapter Sixteen

My head was splitting. I was still having trouble breathing. As I tried to wiggle my arms back and forth, Carrie, tied up beside me, whispered, "Easy, Kyle. Trust me, you are not getting those knots undone. Aly and I have been fiddling with them for the last twenty minutes. Samir is apparently just as good of a tier of knots as he is a fighter."

I breathed a heavy sigh and said, "I blew it, Sis, I am so sorry. Thanks to me, you two are going to die, and mom and dad, and everyone else, too."

"Kyle," Aly whispered in response, "you did what you could, which is more than most anyone else could have done. But aren't you forgetting something?"

"What, sis," I said with a bit of frustration, "what am I forgetting? We are tied up, the bomb is ticking down, Samir is happily sitting there listening to music on his phone, of all things, probably 'The Joy Bells of Jihad,' the evil captain and the other two conspirators are lurking about down here, coming in and out to gloat, and we have been beaten. So, what am I forgetting?"

"You are forgetting our power source, big brother."

Ouch. She was right. Were we tied up and helpless? Yes. Was God tied up and helpless? No.

And so, we prayed. We poured out our hearts for ourselves, mom and dad, and everyone else. If God did not intervene, everyone was going to die...

Including the guy who just slid past us, out cold and with a badly busted nose.

The Captain.

Shocked, we just looked at each other. But if the sight of the captain sliding past us with a broken nose was shocking, what we saw next made that seem ordinary by comparison.

And all of it happened in mere seconds.

One of the guards rushed in and was immediately met by a familiar sized seven and a half ladies' shoe being planted into his, um, "family jewels." He doubled over in agony, and

106

I saw my out-of-control, furious mom beating him into probably permanent unconsciousness. The other guard made it no farther than the end of my dad's next right cross and crumpled onto the ground like a sack of potatoes.

Mom and Dad! What in the world! How were they even here?!?

I did not have time to ask. Samir did not allow that time.

As dad whirled from the guy he had just decked, Samir was instantly on top of him with a hard right hook to the side of the head. Dad caught sight of it coming out of the side of his eye and threw up a left hand to block it. The blow knocked him down anyway, and Samir moved in for the kill. But as fast as a lightning bolt, dad shot back up with an uppercut that caught him right under the jaw. It sounded like a gun had gone off.

Samir was knocked back a few feet and stood there shaking the cobwebs out of his head for a second. And then I heard my dad speak, calmly but confidently.

"Hello, Samir. It seems my kids found your bomb first. My apologies; their sleuthing was better than mine. But now, since it is fighting time, why don't you bring your jihad right on over here and see how well that goes for you?"

How? How did dad know? What all did he know?

Carrie and Aly and I just looked back and forth at each other in amazement. There was clearly going to be a lot of explaining that had to go on later, assuming we survived all of this.

Mom was done beating her guard and had come over to us to try and free us. When she quickly realized she could not get us loose, she simply turned to protect us. But all of us knew that if dad did not win, there would be no protecting us.

Samir smiled back at dad and then began to unbutton his shirt to get down to just his undershirt to make his movements more free. As he took off his shirt, I gasped. This. Guy. Was. Ripped.

But so was dad, I knew that. Samir probably outweighed him by at least thirty pounds, but dad was still the baddest man I knew. If anybody could beat this jerk, it was dad, especially with his family on the line.

Samir tossed the shirt aside, cracked his knuckles, cracked his neck back and forth, and moved in, both hands at the ready. Man, his arms were huge!

"Beat him like a toy drum, dad!" Aly shouted.

"I intend to do just that, Sweetie," he said calmly.

Samir lunged with that vicious left jab. Dad smoothly stepped to his left, brushed the jab aside with his left forearm, and came around with a round kick toward Samir's mid-section. He landed that squarely in the big man's rib cage, causing him to grunt, but not much else.

Dad and Samir began to circle each other. Samir was angry but wary. He clearly was not used to fighting anyone anywhere near his size, skill, and power.

Samir faked a jab and then jumped into a head-high round kick. Dad blocked it, but it was so powerful that he went tumbling to the floor from the impact. Samir rushed to finish him, but dad was instantly up into a crouched position, and he launched himself into the dirt bag's stomach. He wrapped his arms around him, grabbed both of his legs as he did, and drove him into the floor. Samir "oofed," and then slung dad off to the side, and they were quickly both back up again.

Suddenly the punches started coming fast and furious. They were standing toe-to-toe unloading punches in flurries; it seemed that neither of the two had any thought of defense at that moment, it was just a matter of pounding the other into the deck of the ship.

That went on for probably twenty seconds. We were all screaming for dad to get him, but then suddenly, Samir landed an absolutely brutal left hook that exploded into the right side of dad's face. We saw blood spatter everywhere, and dad went down to a knee. Samir smiled that evil smile again and raised both fists high in the air. He was about to bring both of them crashing down onto the back of dad's head!

He exploded downward with a "whoosh" ...

And suddenly, both hands stopped dead. Dad, still on a knee, had reached up and grabbed both of Samir's wrists, stopping his fists in mid-air without even looking up.

The big man was stunned – and angry. He tried to push down, he tried to jerk back, but it was like dad had him in a vise grip.

"I am finished with you, Samir. And now I am going to beat you into the ground for touching my children."

Suddenly dad let go with his left hand and swung a hard chop into the side of Samir's knee, crumpling him to dad's level. Then dad head-butted him in the nose, shattering it, and blood spattered everywhere.

Samir fell back and then leaped back up with a busted nose, hobbling on his now injured knee. Dad was instantly up, his right eye swollen shut and bleeding, but with enough anger in his left eye to scare the daylights out of the devil himself.

Samir threw a right hook. Dad moved into it sideways, blocked it with both arms, grabbed it with his right, stepped back, and shot a vicious side kick into his ribs. Then as he doubled over in pain from that, dad stepped in with a brutal left hook to the side of his face, followed it up with a right uppercut, another left, a right hook, and then with Samir reeling, he pushed him up against the wall, held him in place with his left arm, and ripped seven straight right hands into the man's face.

The only reason there was not an eighth was because Samir crumpled to the ground, unconscious.

.

Chapter Seventeen

Exhausted, dad took a couple of steps back, bent over, put both of his hands on his knees, and said, "I am getting too old for this."

Then he reached down to Samir, pulled the knife out of his sheath, and said, "I'm glad in the heat of the fight he was too arrogant to reach for this. His pride was his undoing; I was barely able to handle him hand to hand, I would have had no chance at all with his power behind this knife."

He quickly cut us loose, and mom hugged us and started to cry. That's my mom; in the heat of the moment, she defeats a full-grown man, then when everything is over she cries.

"Honey, I need you to let them go, especially Kyle. We have a huge issue to deal with, and I need him."

I knew what he meant, but he said it anyway.

"Son," he said as he walked over and tugged on the bomb, "this thing, as I suspected, weighs at least 500 pounds. There is no way I can handle this on my own, I need your help.

"I am going to assume your plan was the same as ours; carry it up on deck and toss it overboard, correct?"

"Yes, sir, that was what we had in mind. But..."

"Not now, son, we will deal with all of that later. Look at that timer. We have just over six minutes. We need to move, right now."

I nodded my head in agreement.

"Babe, you and the girls go ahead of us. Make sure every elevator and door is open, and keep everyone out of our way. Throw more of those 'instant soprano kicks' if necessary."

Aly giggled at that. "Yeah, mom, and we are definitely going to want to talk about that later, m'kay?"

Mom just grinned, and the three of them rushed out to clear a pathway for us.

"Okay, son, here's what we need to do," dad said as he grabbed two long gear bars hanging on a wall nearby. "Slide these bars under the top frame of this bomb casement. Then we are going to crouch down underneath them and lift with our legs. This will be too much for us to handle if we do not lift right, and the legs are the most powerful part of the body."

I nodded in agreement. My dad, the powerlifter, knows what he is talking about when it comes to lifting heavy things.

We put the bars in place, dad got in back, and I got in the front.

"Okay, son, we lift on the count of three. One, two, three."

We both grunted and pushed upward. Oh my goodness, this thing was a pig! After what seemed like forever, we were finally completely upright.

"Good, son, good. Just like a simple squat. Now, we walk together, left leg first, on my mark, one step at a time.

"Left. Right. Left. Right. Left..."

Little by little, we moved. The timer on the bomb seemed not to care about our predicament and simply marched on inexorably.

We made our way out of the room and turned to go back down the corridor. One step at a time, little by little, panting and sweating, we made our way one excruciating step at a time up the flight of stairs, dad actually lifted the back end over his head to keep my end level,

115

and then we finally reached the elevator. Mom and the girls were keeping the doors open for us, and we could hear the elevator beeping in protest.

We got us and the bomb inside, pushed the button for the very top floor, and the doors closed behind us.

"I need to set this thing down for a second, dad," I said as my legs began to shake.

"No, Kyle. I know you are hurting and tired, but if we set this thing down, you will never get it up again. Girls, hold the sides toward the front, take some of the weight off of him, please."

Mom and the girls came to me, mom on one side and Carrie and Aly on the other, and they lifted up with all their might. I could feel my load lighten instantly.

"Thank you, thank you a bunch," I breathed out heavily.

They just nodded, concentrating on lifting.

After what seemed like an eternity, we reached the top deck, and the doors slid open. I looked at the timer, and in a panic said, "Fifty-five seconds!"

We started out of the elevator, and someone screamed "bomb!" and pointed at us. Instantly people began to shriek and to run in every direction except where we were. In seconds there was literally no one on deck but us.

"What good do they think that is going to do them?" Carrie asked in bewilderment. "If this thing blows, everyone on the boat is dead, no matter where in the boat they are!"

"People don't think clearly when they are panicking, babe," dad grunted. "Now come on, Kyle, hurry to the back of the boat!

Our attempt to run carrying that weight was nothing more than a shuffle, really, but it was a fast shuffle.

"Forty seconds!" I shouted as we passed the pool.

"Thirty seconds!" as we passed the putt-putt course.

"I hate this course," Aly said as we did. I would have won if my ball hadn't bounced out."

"Really, sis? You have to bring that up now?!? Twenty seconds!!!"

We sped up as much as we could. We reached the edge of the deck at ten seconds.

"Everybody, hoist and push up!" dad screamed, and five Warners gave the mightiest heave they could with every ounce of strength left in their weary bodies.

The bomb went over the edge. Dad grabbed me, mom grabbed the girls, and they threw us backward to the deck and landed on top of us.

Chapter Eighteen

Dad looked horrible as he sat across from me at the table slowly sipping his unsweet tea. His eye was as black as soot and so puffy I knew the swelling would not go down for days. He had seven stitches on his cheek.

"That man hits really hard," he said matter of factly.

Mom was hovering all over us, taking care of every little bruise and scrape. The side of Aly's face was badly swollen, and yet, she thought it was the coolest thing in the world.

"Wook ah mi," she giggled, "ah wook wike Wocky Bowboa."

Carrie was holding a bag of ice on her nose. She lowered it long enough to point at it and say, "Um, Rocky, meet Rudolph!"

They both laughed.

"Sir, ma'am," the co-pilot said as he approached us at the table, "I wanted to come by and thank you again for what all of you did. That was way too close. From the way that bomb lifted the entire back half of the ship out of the water when it went off, if it had blown up down where you found it, I can assure you that it would have ripped the entire ship in half. She would have gone down literally in seconds; no one on board would have stood a chance of survival.

"Can I do anything at all for any of you?"

"No, sir, I believe we are just fine," dad said. "I am just glad we were able to do what needed to be done."

"Well," the co-pilot, actually the acting captain now, said, "you will be glad to know that all four of the conspirators are safely locked up, and homeland security is actually on the way here now to get them. I just can't believe it was Captain Ali; he always seemed like the nicest man in the world, we have worked together for years.

"Oh, and you will also be pleased to know that corporate office called, and in thanks for what you fine folks have done, they want to offer you a free cruise next year on any of our ships to any destination of your choice."

Dad choked and spit out his tea and gagged to catch his breath.

"Sorry, I apologize for that," he said, "but, um, if its all the same to you, we'll pass. Our next several vacations will be on land, preferably so far inland that only peaceful senior citizens even know where it is."

"I understand, sir," he laughed. "Well, until we arrive back at port, if you have need of anything at all, please let me know."

And then he nodded to us and walked away. When he did and I knew we were out of earshot of anyone else, I turned to mom and dad. I wanted to be very careful in what I said. I did not know what they knew, and I did not want to give anything away needlessly.

"Dad, um," I began, "um, how did you know to come looking for us, and how did you find us?"

He smiled. "Well, to be honest, we did not know you three were wrapped up in any of this until we heard Aly scream 'Man overboard!' That was a bit of a shock to us, especially since that is what we planned on doing."

"What seriously?!?" Aly squealed.

"Yes, sweetie, seriously," mom nodded. "Our 'body' is still up in our room. You beat us to the drop by about two minutes. By the way, we named our victim 'Chuck,' as in 'chuck him overboard.' What did you name yours?"

"WHAATTTT?!? You named your body, and we didn't?!? Agggghhhh! How could we have missed that?" She shrieked accusingly at Carrie and me.

I just got wide-eyed and shrugged an "I don't know" shrug.

"Anyway," dad said, "your mom and I have been on the trail of those guys since the first night at supper. The way Samir acted toward our prayer troubled me so very badly. When we got back to the room later, I spoke to your mom about it, and she felt the same way.

"And then when she and I were praying together later that night, we both seemed to feel the Holy Spirit nudge us to go 'poke around.' As we did, we passed by a chapel, and for some reason, felt the leading to go inside. When we did, we found a copy of the Koran wrapped up on the shelf. I picked it up and opened it, and found a map inside, a map of our cruising route.

"I also found a rather odd detour on that route. We would, for no good reason, swing over the Puerto Rico Trench. That is many miles out of the way and is notable for only one thing—it is the deepest spot in the entire Atlantic Ocean. 5.2 miles deep, in fact.

"Add that to the fact that Samir, whom I went and trailed during the supper I skipped out on, was busy up on deck practicing with a camera drone, and the fact that today is the date of the anniversary of the day Osama Bin Laden was buried at sea, and we just sort of put two and two together."

I was stunned. Who knew mom and dad had that kind of "Night Hero" skills about them?

"But that begs another question, Kyle Warner."

Uh oh. I knew what was coming. The first and last name thing was a dead giveaway.

"What in the world were my three children, whom it is my job to keep safe, doing chasing after terrorists? Did you not think that maybe, just maybe you should have come to us about that? I have a very good mind to...

"to...

"to..."

We just looked at him. He was half-way like a broken record, and half-way like he was listening to something. Or to Someone.

"Never mind. Forget I asked," he said with a faint smile. "Just promise me that you three will always take care of each other, okay?"

Carrie and Aly and I just looked at each other. Then we looked at mom, and she had her head bowed and her eyes closed. We looked at dad, and he had a look on his face that it is almost impossible to describe. It was a look that prompted we Night Heroes to look at each other later that night in our room and say,

"How much do you think they know?"

Coming Soon

Winter Wolf

The heavy, fast-falling snow was oh, so cold. But nowhere near as cold as the dozen or so rifle barrels pointing right at us.

"If you want to try and keep this baby alive, then take it and go. But under no circumstances can it stay with us a single minute longer. The more it cries, the more of these wolves keep coming, especially that ungodly monster leading the pack. Enough of these men have died already, and no one else among us is going to do so if I can help it."

I looked over at Carrie and Aly and immediately had my answer. The looks on their faces as they mothered that precious, helpless babe let me know that we would save it or die trying.

So come on ahead, wolf; the Night Heroes will be ready for you.

Other Books by Dr. Bo Wagner

Beyond the Colored Coat
Daniel: Breathtaking
Don't Muzzle the Ox
Esther: Five Feast and the Finger Prints of God
From Footers to Finish Nails
I'm Saved! Now What???
James: The Pen and the Plumb Line
Jonah: A Study in Greatness
Marriage Makers/Marriage Breakers
Nehemiah: A Labor of Love
Romans: Salvation From A-Z
Ruth: Diamonds in the Darkness
DO Drops Volume 1
Do Drops Volume 2

Fiction Titles

Night Heroes Series:
Cry From the Coal Mine (Vol. 1)
Free Fall (Vol. 2)
Broken Brotherhood (Vol. 3)
The Blade of Black Crow (Vol. 4)
Ghost Ship (Vol. 5)
When Serpents Rise (Vol. 6)
Moth Man (Vol. 7)
Runaway (Vol. 8)

Sci-Fi

Zak Blue and the Great Space Chase Series:
Falcon Wing (Vol. 1)